I Am a S

by Jessica Pippin • illustrated by Juan Bautista Juan Oliver

Gram and I always sing together.

We know all the latest songs.

One day I was singing at school.

"Can I talk to you, Jovan?"
asked Mr. Brian.

"Family Night is coming up," he said.

"Would you like to sing a solo?"

"What's a solo?" I asked.

"It's when you sing by yourself," he explained.

When I got home, I told Gram,
"I'm going to be a star!"

"That's wonderful!" she exclaimed.
She helped me practice every night.

Finally, Family Night came!

"What if I forget the words?" I asked Gram.

"You've practiced really hard," said Gram.

"Just do your best."

"Pretend you are singing
for me at home," she said.

So I closed my eyes and imagined
myself singing my best.

We all went onstage.

It was time for my solo.

I sang as loudly as I could.

Everyone cheered and clapped.

Gram yelled out, "You're my star!"